CAPTAIN AWESOME
vs. Nacho Cheese Man

By STAN KIRBY   Illustrated by GEORGE O'CONNOR

LITTLE SIMON
New York London Toronto Sydney New Delhi

ABDO
Spotlight

ABDOPUBLISHING.COM

Reinforced library bound edition published in 2019 by Spotlight, a division of ABDO, PO Box 398166, Minneapolis, Minnesota 55439. Spotlight produces high-quality reinforced library bound editions for schools and libraries. Published by agreement with Little Simon.

Printed in the United States of America, North Mankato, Minnesota.
042018
092018

THIS BOOK CONTAINS RECYCLED MATERIALS

 LITTLE SIMON

An imprint of Simon & Schuster Children's Publishing Division
1230 Avenue of the Americas, New York, New York 10020

Library of Congress Control Number: 2017961019

Publisher's Cataloging in Publication Data

Names: Kirby, Stan, author. | O'Connor, George, illustrator.
Title: Captain Awesome vs. Nacho Cheese Man / by Stan Kirby; illustrated by George O'Connor.
Description: Minneapolis, MN : Spotlight, 2019 | Series: Captain Awesome; #2
Summary: Eugene and Charlie, aka Captain Awesome and Nacho Cheese Man, get into a huge fight, but as the boys learn how to sort out the good guys and the bad guys, they also learn about friendship and what it means to be a superhero.
Identifiers: ISBN 9781532142000 (lib. bdg.)
Subjects: LCSH: Kirby, Stan. Captain Awesome--Juvenile fiction. | Superheroes--Juvenile fiction. | Best friends--Juvenile fiction. | Lost and found possessions--Juvenile fiction. | Comic books, strips, etc.--Juvenile fiction.
Classification: DDC [E]--dc23

Spotlight
A Division of ABDO
abdopublishing.com

Table of Contents

CHAPTER I

The Slobbering Power of Mr. Drools

By Eugene

"**B**y the super MI-TEE force of Captain Awesome and the canned cheese power of Nacho Cheese Man, I call this Sunnyview Superhero Squad tree house sleepover meeting to order."

THUMP!

Eugene McGillicudy banged a wooden spoon against an empty shoebox. The Sunnyview Superhero Squad meeting had begun.

Sunnyview? Superhero? Squad?

That's right! Eugene and his best friend Charlie Thomas Jones were not just ordinary students at Sunnyview Elementary. They also had super secret superhero identities. Eugene was **Captain Awesome** and Charlie was **Nacho Cheese Man.**

Together, along with Captain Awesome's hamster sidekick (and the class pet), **Turbo**, they formed the Sunnyview Superhero Squad to protect the universe from bad guys.

"Hurry up," Charlie said. "The brownies are waiting!"

Brownies! Yum! The perfect superhero snack! thought Eugene. Evil doesn't stand a chance against chocolate fudge.

The first thing to do was to thank Eugene's mom, Betsy, for the home-made brownies and milk that she brought to the tree house. The next order of business was to eat them!

"Thanks, Mom," Eugene said, his mouth stuffed full of brownie.

"Thmph, Mmphs Mmmklldph," Charlie mumbled, trying not to dribble any on his Super Dude T-shirt.

"You're welcome, Charlie . . . I think," Eugene's mom said. Having delivered her sweet superhero treats, she climbed back down the ladder.

She knew that when it came to saving the world from the bad guys, it was always best for moms and dads to leave it to the experts: Captain Awesome and Nacho Cheese Man!

The Sunnyview Superhero Squad had one mission: **to stop the evily spread of evil in Sunnyview.** Their one mission, however, had three parts.

1. Be alert to evil.
2. Find evil.
3. Stop evil from eviling.

"I think we should add part number four: Eat more brownies!" Charlie quickly stuffed another brownie into his mouth.

"All those in favor of our mission—"

Charlie raised his hand. "Ambd meefing mrr mrownees?"

"Yes, Nacho Cheese Man. Including 'Eat more brownies,'" Eugene replied. "Those in favor, say the super word of the day!"

"MI-TEE!" Eugene and Charlie said at the same time. Even Turbo let out a little squeak.

Eugene banged the wooden spoon against the shoe box again. **THUMP! THUMP! THUMP!** It was time for the Squad's main non–evil-stopping activity (besides eating more brownies): reading the latest issue of Super Dude!

"Issue number four hundred twenty-nine!" Charlie cheered.

"Only the greatest thing since issue number four hundred twenty-eight!" Eugene declared.

Each member of the Sunnyview Superhero Squad . . . Wait. What's that you say? You've never heard of Super Dude? You're not a member of FsssDsss, the Friends of Super Dude Society, like Eugene and Charlie? You don't know about his TV show, toys, games, action figures, and more? Where do you live? The Moon?!

Super Dude is only the most

amazing superhero of all time. Just listen!

Eugene opened the comic. "Page one: Super Dude's archnemesis Trash Can't was back in Super City. 'I'm ready to crush Super Dude and trash his inner dudeness.'"

"Whoa. This is going to be the greatest issue ever!" Eugene could barely wait to turn the page!

And it was! Just when it looked like Super Dude would lose for sure and Trash Can't would litter his evil garbageness across the world,

Super Dude punched Trash Can't right in the recycling bin and dumped him on the curb in time for trash day.

Eugene turned the last page and closed the comic. He and Charlie sat in silence.

"That was the greatest thing I've ever read," Eugene finally said with a sigh, still in awe. "This is, without a doubt, my most favorite comic book . . . ever! No. Make that double-ever!"

"Whoa. The only thing I've *ever* double-evered was peanut-butter-fudge nachos with marshmallows. You know, the tiny ones?" Charlie said.

With the latest awesome issue of Super Dude completed, Eugene rubbed Turbo's furry head. "Good night, buddy."

"Good night, Turbo," Charlie said and clicked off his flashlight.

Soon both heroes were fast asleep and the tree house was filled with the squeak of Turbo's exercise

wheel as it spun round and round.

Then there was a **_BUMP!_**
Eugene opened one sleepy eye.

That's probably nothing.

Then he heard it again. **_THUMP!_**
His other eye snapped open.

That's something. My Captain Awesome Danger Sense is tingling!

Something was in the yard. Eugene sat up in his sleeping bag and listened. **_RATTLE!_**

Could it be?!

"GRRRRR! ROWL! SNARL!"

Yes, it was! His old furry enemy **Mr. Drools** had returned! Mr. Drools was the hairy four-legged monster from the Howling Paw Nebula whose drooly jaws

loved to chomp everything Eugene held most dear.

And worse, his evil Drool House was right next door to Eugene's home. Mr. Drools had turned the once normal house into his own "barkyard."

He's stolen three Frisbees, popped my soccer ball, eaten the cover off my baseball, and ripped up my kite like an old sock! What's he after this time?! Eugene wondered. Then he realized something awful. . . . *NOOOOOOOOO! NOT MY SUPER DUDE ISSUE No. 429!?*

Eugene jumped up without unzipping his sleeping bag. He hopped like the rare hopping cater-pillars of Mothonia in Super Dude

No. 97. He hopped on his flashlight, lost his balance, and fell to the wooden floor.

Eugene crawled from his sleeping bag.

Splinter!

"Ouch! Ouch! Ouch!"

Since superheroes can do anything, Eugene quickly pulled out the splinter. He felt around for his flashlight and clicked it on.

This was a nighttime job for Captain Awesome and Nacho Cheese Man!

"Wake up!" he whispered to

Charlie. "Mr. Drools is in his barkyard next door!"

Charlie shot out of his sleeping bag like he'd been stuck with a pin. He grabbed the emergency can of nacho cheese he kept under his pillow.

Eugene placed Turbo into the Turbomobile. They would need the power of two heroes and one sidekick to stop the barking, slobbery madness of Mr. Drools.

"Go chase your tail, Mr. Drools! You'll never get my comic book!"

Captain Awesome called down from the tree house. "Your slobber is useless on this night!"

"I must warn you now . . ." Nacho Cheese Man called out. "I've got cheese!"

The trio of heroes climbed down from their tree house moon base and onto the cold surface of the Moon. . . .

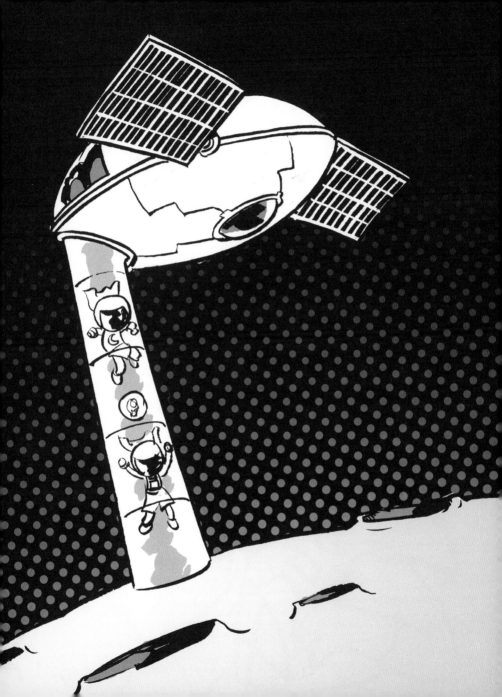

CHAPTER 2

Fighting Evil Is Messy

By Eugene

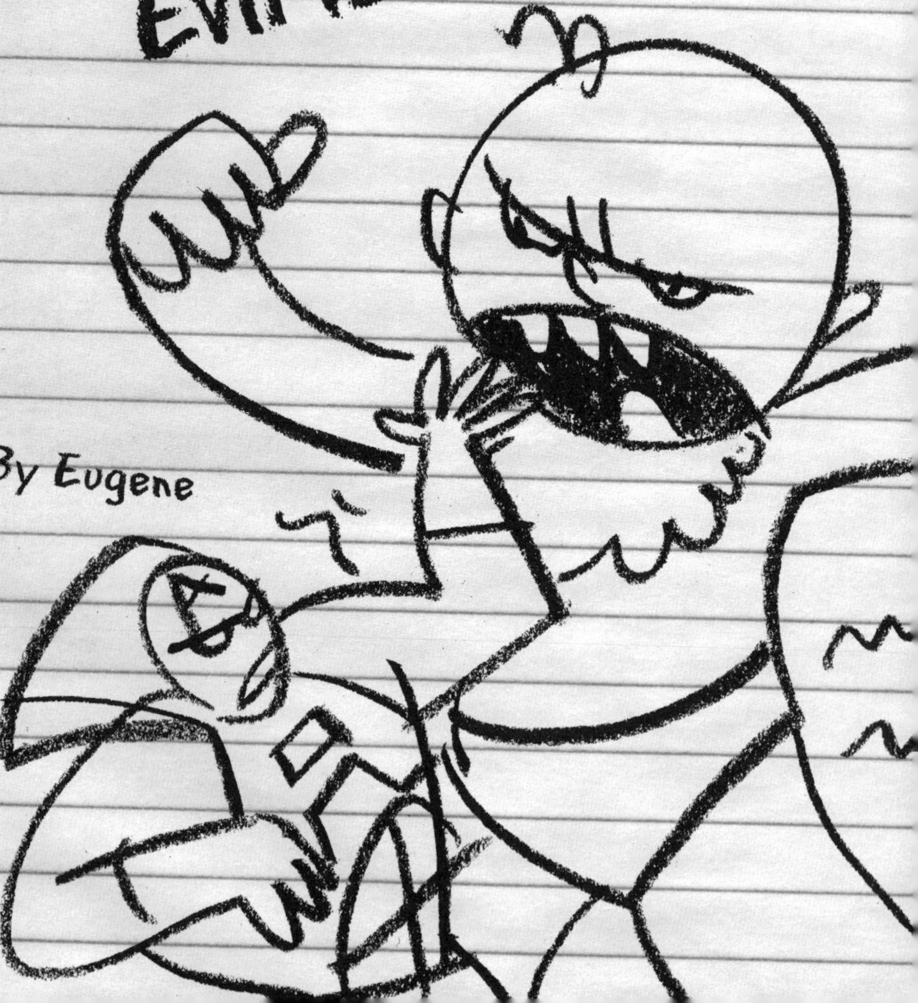

"**W**hat a mess!" Charlie said as he stood in the middle of Eugene's backyard the next morning. He picked up a can of cheese and shook it. Empty.

"That's just one of the many problems with evil." Eugene picked up an old banana peel and dropped it into the trash can. "It never picks up after itself."

Mr. Drools had gotten away. He escaped thanks to his Doggie Door of Droolness, but he'd return. The bad guys always do.

Eugene's mom smiled as the boys came into the house. "Here you go, boys. Super Dude-O's, the breakfast of the world's greatest superhero."

In many ways Eugene's mom

was a hero
too. She didn't wear a cape
or fight evil, but her ongoing battle
against cavities, late homework,
and tantrums was almost as important as saving the world. Almost.
Plus she always whipped up awesome breakfasts to make Eugene
superhero strong.

The two boys ate faster than

Sir Snacksalot who once challenged Super Dude to an eating contest. Super Dude won by eating fried okra.

After breakfast Charlie headed to his house down the street, and Eugene returned to his backyard. The moment he turned the corner, his nose was instantly filled with the stinky stink of stink!

"YUCK! THE STINKY STINK OF STINK!" Eugene gasped.

"GROSS!" Eugene held his nose.

Eugene didn't have to smell another stink bomb to know what was up.

It was **Queen Stinkypants** from Planet Baby! Her Dangerous Diaper of Doom was packed with stinky diaper awfulness.

"Gaa-baa-boo," she said in her alien baby language as she waddled across Eugene's backyard.

She hasn't seen me yet, Eugene thought.

Eugene knew she was up to something. Queen Stinkypants was always up to something.

She walked, fell, crawled, and waddled to the gate. So! She was the one who opened the secret passageway from Mr. Drools's

barkyard to the surface of the Moon. She wanted Mr. Drools to return for the Super Dude comic he didn't get last night.

"Well, not today! Not tonight! Never again, and never ever!" Eugene called out in his awesome Captain Awesome voice.

Eugene ripped off his shirt and revealed . . . that he'd forgotten to put on his Captain Awesome outfit underneath. Brrrr! Cold!

Eugene ran inside the house and grabbed his outfit from the laundry. "Gotta have it, Mom! Danger is all around me! Stinky danger!"

"Danger smells?" his mother asked, smiling.

"It does when it's stinky!" Eugene changed on the run. That meant he crashed into a hall door— **OUCH!**—bounced off a wall— **OOF!**—and then slid across the kitchen floor on his stomach.

whee!

Eugene flung open the screen door.

"Stop, villain!"

Queen Stinkypants turned to face him. "Glyxl?" she threatened.

Captain Awesome did an awesome jump onto the surface of the Moon. **MI-TEE!**

"Stop your eviling and please . . . take a bath!"

CHAPTER 3

The Missing
Comic Book Caper

By Eugene

"Mom! Have you seen it?"

Eugene screeched down the stairs.

"Seen what, dear?"

What? How could she not know the "what" I'm talking about? It's only the most important thing in forever!

Eugene was shocked. Was his

EUGENE'S
SUPER-SECRET
AWESOME
STUFF

mother not aware of Super Dude? Did she not see the posters, the DVDs, the collectible action figures on her son's dresser?

Eugene's bestest, favoritist comic book in his whole collection was not in its special hiding spot in the box under his bed.

It was gone.

Super Dude No. 429 was missing!

Did Mr. Drools sneak into Eugene's room, take Super Dude No. 429 in his giant paws of evil, and run away with it?

Panic began to hit Eugene. The thought was too horrible to imagine! All that drool all over Super Dude!

"And I double-evered that issue!"

He checked his bedroom floor. No muddy footprints. No bite marks on the door. No fleas hopping about on Eugene's pillow. No sign that Mr. Drools had made it inside Captain Awesome's secret headquarters.

But the comic book was gone. And someone had taken it. No one had been in his room except . . .

Aw, BARF! I showed my comic to Charlie when we were in the tree house. But no member of

the Sunnyview Superhero Squad
would do anything bad . . . right?

Right?

Eugene slumped. He missed
his comic book so much he was
even thinking his best friend took
it. That was the worst thought he
had ever had . . . except for the
one about the drool being all over
Super Dude.

CHAPTER 4

Turbo Day

By Eugene

"Turbo! Turbo! Turbo!"

The class chanted the name of their pet hamster. It was Thursday and that meant it was Turbo Day. As Turbo's caretaker, Eugene made sure to get him to school early.

In Ms. Beasley's second-grade classroom, Turbo Day meant a celebration of everything Turbo.

You only need two things to have Turbo Day:

1) Turbo

2) A Day

If there's one thing that would cheer up Eugene, it was Turbo Day. And it would give him a chance to check Charlie's cubby for the missing comic book.

Y'know. Just in case.

"Turbo! Turbo! Turbo! Who's the hamster on the go? It's Turbo!" The class sang a special cheer written just for Turbo.

The class was distracted by Turbo's cuteness and good hamster manners. Now was Eugene's chance! He wandered to the back of the room. No one was looking.

No Super Dude comic. But he did find a few half-empty cans of cheese.

If Charlie was the thief, he was more clever than Commander Nylon, who kept stealing Super Dude's socks while he was sleeping and used them to stitch a humongous sock monster.

Eugene snuck back to the circle just in time for the Turbo game. Turbo rolled around the floor in his plastic ball showing off his athletic skills.

Awesome. Look at him go! What a good little sidekick! Eugene proudly thought.

The class squealed and cheered with delight. Turbo Day was a success!

"Turbo Force . . . now!" Eugene called out to Turbo.

Everyone will be impressed when Turbo rolls right to me just like he always does. Eugene smiled at the thought.

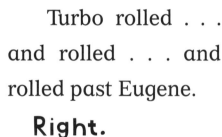

Turbo rolled . . . and rolled . . . and rolled past Eugene.

Right.
    Past.
        Eugene.

WHAT?! Where's he going? Turbo rolled to . . .

Charlie? **GAHHH!** This is worse than the time that Super Squirrel bit Super Dude's super finger when Super Dude fed him that Super Acorn from the Super Oak Tree!

"Charlie?" Eugene called out. "Why did Turbo roll right to you?"

Charlie shrugged. "I don't know, but that was cool, huh?" Charlie patted the top of the hamster ball and carried it over to Turbo's cage.

What's going on here? My favorite comic book in forever is missing and now my faithful side-kick has Turbo Forced to somebody else?

Eugene quickly looked around the classroom to see if anyone was using a mind-control hat. There could be no other explanation. But there was no one with a mind-control hat. Eugene realized there *must* be another explanation.

There must be. . . .

CHAPTER 5

The Evilest Field Trip of All

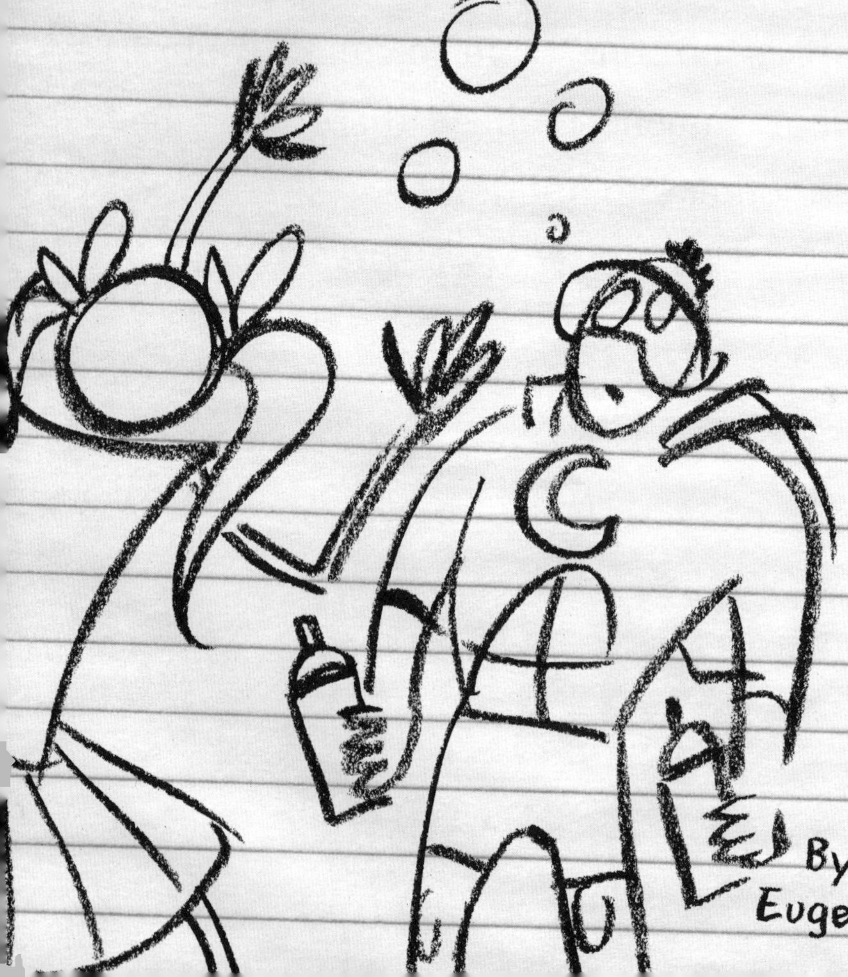

By Eugene

"Okay, everyone," Ms. Beasley called out. "Let's get moving!"

The best thing about school that isn't Turbo Day is a class field trip. Eugene couldn't wait. If anything could take his mind off his missing comic, it would be a trip to the zoo. He loved field trips. If you asked Eugene what his favorite class was in school, his answer would be field trip.

His *second* favorite class?

"Another field trip."

And a trip to the zoo would also give Eugene a chance to see if there was any crime or bad stuff happening in Sunnyview. Plus he'd see some pretty cool animals.

As his classmates filed out of the classroom, Eugene pretended to tie his shoelace. After the class was empty, he scampered to Charlie's desk and searched through his things. Books. Pencils. A ruler. Cans of cheese. But still no sign of Super Dude No. 429.

Maybe I'm wrong about Charlie. But who else could've taken my comic?

"Eugene? Are you coming?" Ms. Beasley asked, poking her head back into the classroom.

"Coming!" Eugene raced for the door. He'd be the last one on the bus, but that was no problem.

Charlie would save a seat for him like he always did.

You can always count on a superhero best friend.

Eugene raced up the steps and onto the bus. He now felt silly for thinking his best friend, Charlie, had taken his comic book. He couldn't wait to sit next to him for the long ride to the zoo.

And then the world turned upside down! Eugene's mouth hit the floor! He saw the most horrible thing he could ever possibly see except for that time his dad gave him a haircut.

Meredith Mooney was sitting next to Charlie. Not Eugene . . . Meredith. *The awful "ME . . . MY . . . MEREDITH!"*

ARGH!

"Hey, Charlie!" Eugene said. "I thought you were saving me a seat?"

"I got here first." Meredith smiled.

"Sorry, Eugene," Charlie said. "She did call 'firsties.'"

DOUBLE *ARGH!* What kind of person steals a seat on a bus? And what kind of a best friend lets a seat stealer call "firsties"?!

Seat-stealing is just the kind of thing a supervillain does when they're not trying to crush the world or steal radioactive waste from the Moon!

This was not Meredith Mooney, the girl who always wore pink ribbons in her hair. This was **Little Miss Stinky Pinky**, the sworn enemy of Captain Awesome, and no friend to his sidekick, Turbo, either. She had once hamsternapped him. Nacho Cheese Man knew she was bad, even if she did wear pink ribbons in her hair.

But what was her evil plan?

Villains like Little Miss Stinky Pinky were always up to no good!

Maybe she was trying to get information out of Charlie. Or WORSE! WORSER THAN WORSE! Maybe she was trying to crush the Sunnyview Superhero Squad? Evil hates best friend superheroes!

"There's a seat up here, Eugene," Ms. Beasley called out and patted the empty seat next to her.

Sit next to the teacher on a field trip?

BARF!

That's even worse than sitting next to your sister or getting cheek-pinched by wrinkly old Aunt Matilda!

What kind of Superhero Squad member is Nacho Cheese Man? Eugene wondered as he made the long, doomed journey to the seat next to Ms. Beasley. If he can't be counted on to battle all super-villains calling "firsties," what'll he do when a supervillain blasts the Earth with melted butter? *Nacho*

Cheese Man is no longer on the side of goodness and hamsters. He did steal my comic, I'll bet!

It was time now for Captain Awesome to confront a new, cheesy evil!

"You might not be able to stand up against bus seat firsties," Eugene said quietly. **"But keep your cheesy hands off my comic books!"**

CHAPTER 6

Beware of the No-Good, Rotten, Gunky, Stink Egg, Monkey-Faced Potato, Evil Alien Robot Brain from Outer Space!

By Eugene

Charlie rocked back and forth on his swing, trying to move. He wobbled, weebled and wobbled, then wobbled some more. No luck. He wasn't going anywhere. The thing about swings is, if you can't get going on your own, then it's really just like sitting in a chair with chains.

"It's your turn to push," Charlie finally said to

Eugene, who sat on the swing next to him.

Eugene didn't reply. He just scrunched his face up like he was pretending to be a prune.

"Eugene? It's your turn to—"

"NO WAY!" The words just exploded from Eugene's mouth.

Eugene jumped from his swing, looking more scrunchy and prune-faced than ever before and stomped to Charlie.

"Listen! CAPTAIN AWESOME is the leader of the Sunnyview Superhero Squad, NOT Nacho

Cheese Head!"

"Nacho Cheese *Man*," Charlie corrected, a little annoyed.

"And since CAPTAIN AWE-SOME is the leader of the Super-

hero Squad and NOT Nacho
Bologna Head, you should be
pushing *me* on the swings!" Eugene
continued.

Now it was Charlie's turn to be
quiet. He didn't know what to say
or why Eugene was acting like he
was. Then it hit him! Aliens stole
his best friend's brain, stuck it in

a jar, and replaced it with an evil alien robot brain!

Charlie leaped from his swing! "Don't worry, Captain Awesome!" He used his heroic Nacho Cheese Man voice. "I'll save your brain!"

"*And* I know *you* stole my most favorite, best Super Dude comic book ever!"

"I did not!" Charlie said, defending himself.

"Did so! Issue number four hundred twenty-nine! You were there when I double-evered it!" Eugene said. "And you teamed up with the worstest, most evil, and pinkest supervillain in the whole biggest universe to do it: Little Miss Stinky Pinky!" *Gross!*

"You . . . you don't really mean that?" Charlie was stunned.

"I mean it like my mom does when she says 'eat your vegetables or you won't get any dessert,'" Eugene growled.

Charlie's stomach twisted into knots and he felt sick—and not just because Eugene was talking about vegetables. "I was wrong," Charlie began. "Aliens didn't switch your brain with an evil alien robot brain . . . they switched it with a **NO-GOOD, ROTTEN, GUNKY, STINK EGG, MONKEY-FACED POTATO, EVIL ALIEN ROBOT BRAIN!**"

Charlie stomped off, then turned around. "And I never stole your stupid comic book!" Charlie stomped off, then turned around again. "And I quit the Superhero Squad!"

Charlie stomped off, but this time, there was no more turning around.

Eugene plopped back onto the swing and crossed his arms. He was angrier than the time Queen Stinkypants flushed his Super Dude action figure down the toilet. And in fact Eugene would've been a lot more angry . . . if he wasn't so sad.

CHAPTER 7

I Don't Feel Like Dessert.

By Eugene

Eugene sat at the table and stared at his vegetables. He rolled the peas to one side of his plate then rolled them behind the mashed potatoes so he wouldn't have to look at them. Eugene's mom made peas a lot. Sometimes she steamed them. Sometimes she boiled them. Sometimes she added butter. Sometimes she added tiny little onions. But no matter how she tried to disguise the little green things, they were still icky peas! ***BLECH!***

Eugene lifted his mashed potatoes with his spoon and mushed them over the peas.

"Eat your vegetables or you won't get any dessert," his mom reminded him.

Eugene sighed. He didn't feel like eating anything anyway, including dessert.

Eugene's mom touched her son's hand. "You seem upset, Eugene. Is something wrong?"

Eugene shrugged and mumbled something that sounded like "Dere's muffin gong."

"I know what might cheer you up," his mom continued. "What if we asked Charlie's mom if Charlie can

come over this Friday for another
sleepover?"

"Charlie's not my best friend!
He's not even my *worst* friend!
I'd rather have a sleepover with
Queen Stinkypants than Charlie

because at least I already know Queen Stinkypants is going to try to shoot me into space in a giant diaper, so it won't be a surprise when she does!"

Eugene raced from the table and ran to his room.

His mom and dad sat at the

table in shocked silence. Then Eugene's dad, Ned, asked, "Wait. Who's Queen Stinkypants?"

"I really think that one of us should go see what's up with him," Eugene's mom said.

"I'll go." Eugene's dad quickly got up from his seat. He hoped that, by the time he came back to the dinner table, his wife would've already thrown away the icky peas he'd hidden under the roast beef on his plate.

CHAPTER 8

Who's the Bad Guy Now?

By Eugene

Eugene's dad knocked on the door. Eugene covered his head with a pillow and mumbled, "Come in."

His dad sat on the bed. "Are you okay, son?" Eugene's dad felt a bit strange talking to a pillow. "Did something happen with Charlie?"

"Everything went wrong with Charlie!" Eugene blurted, throwing the pillow off his face. "Turbo rolled to Charlie and not me when I called 'Turbo Force,' then Charlie let

Meredith Mooney sit next to him on the bus just 'cause she called 'firsties,' and he wanted me to push him on the swing just 'cause it was my turn to push, and most of all he stole my favoritest double-evered

Super Dude number four hundred twenty-nine comic!" Eugene took a deep breath. Saying all those words at once made his face turn really red.

Eugene's dad thought about his son's problems very carefully, mostly because he had no idea what "Turbo Force," "firsties," and "double-evered" even meant, but also because he loved Eugene and didn't want to mess things up even more. Luckily, Eugene's dad knew one way he could help.

"Eugene, I don't think Charlie

stole your Super Dude comic. . . ."

"How would you know that unless you had X-ray vision or something?" Eugene paused for a moment, then asked hopefully, "*Do you have X-ray vision?*"

"No, son, but I do have this. . . ."

Eugene's dad pulled out the missing copy of Super Dude No. 429. Eugene practically fell out of his bed. How did his *dad* get his Super Dude comic!? Was *he* the one who took the comic from Eugene's room!? But *why*?! Then it hit Eugene! Aliens stole his dad's

brain, stuck it in a jar, and replaced it with an evil alien robot brain!

Eugene leaped from his bed! "Don't you worry, Dad! Captain Awesome will save your brain!"

"My brain is fine. Although . . . I do get a little headache sometimes when I see your mom's made more peas for dinner. . . ."

"But why did you take my comic?" If aliens didn't steal his dad's brain . . . well, Eugene was very confused.

"I didn't take it. I found it in Molly's baby doll stroller. And I think she took it because she wanted to play with you. She wanted to do something you liked to do."

She wanted to play *with me?* Eugene thought. "When I saw her in the backyard, I kinda called her a 'bad guy' and told her to not open the doorway to the barkyard," Eugene confessed, feeling rotten.

"Molly was going to open the doorway . . . to the, oh . . . backyard? That *is* pretty serious stuff." Eugene's dad put an arm around his son. The boy stared quietly at the Super Dude comic. "Eugene, do you know what makes Super Dude a *super*hero? It's not the costume or the

superpowers, it's because, when someone needs help, Super Dude does *everything* he can to help them, no matter *who* they are. He treats everyone with kindness and respect—except for the bad guys, of course. And that makes him someone the rest of us can look up to and admire . . . just like Molly does to you, her big brother."

The last words made Eugene have a terrible thought—yes, even more terrible than Super Dude covered in drool. He hadn't been very nice to his little sister, and if she was the one who took his Super Dude comic, then he had been pretty rotten to Charlie as well.

The thought was really hard for Eugene to swallow, even harder than his mom's icky peas. Maybe it was Captain Awesome who was acting like the "bad guy" after all.

CHAPTER 9

Something Better Than Pizza

By
Eugene

The next day at school was Friday.

Pizza Friday!

Pizza Fridays are the most awesome day of the week because, in case you couldn't guess by the name, they served pizza in the cafeteria. Eugene loved it . . . much more than Mystery Meat Mondays.

Actually, Eugene loved almost anything more than Mystery Meat Mondays.

But this Friday, Eugene wasn't very excited about much—even pizza. He took a bite of the cheesy triangle and sighed. Usually, he and Charlie would see who could make the longest cheese string from their mouths to the pizza slice, but making cheese strings wasn't much fun sitting alone.

Charlie was sitting across the cafeteria. He wasn't making cheese strings, either. Eugene picked up

his lunch tray and headed over. Eugene had a lot to say. There was so much to explain, but he left it all up to one word:

"Sorry."

Charlie shrugged and ate his pizza.

Eugene continued. "Captain Awesome didn't—I mean *I* didn't treat you very well and I'm sorry. Will you please come back to the Sunnyview Superhero Squad?"

"Because the safety of the universe kinda depends on it?" Charlie asked.

"No," Eugene replied. "Because you're my best friend."

Charlie smiled. He was about to say something, but made a cheese string instead. "I bet you can't beat that one!"

Eugene bit his pizza. A gooey cheesy cheese string stretched from his mouth to the pizza slice.

The string broke and flopped over Eugene's chin.

"MI-TEE!" Eugene and Charlie said at the same time.

The two boys laughed and their happiness washed away any bad feelings over their fight.

So bad guys beware! Nacho Cheese Man and Captain Awesome were back. The Sunnyview Superhero Squad was together again!

And just in time for a sleepover on Friday night.

CHAPTER 10

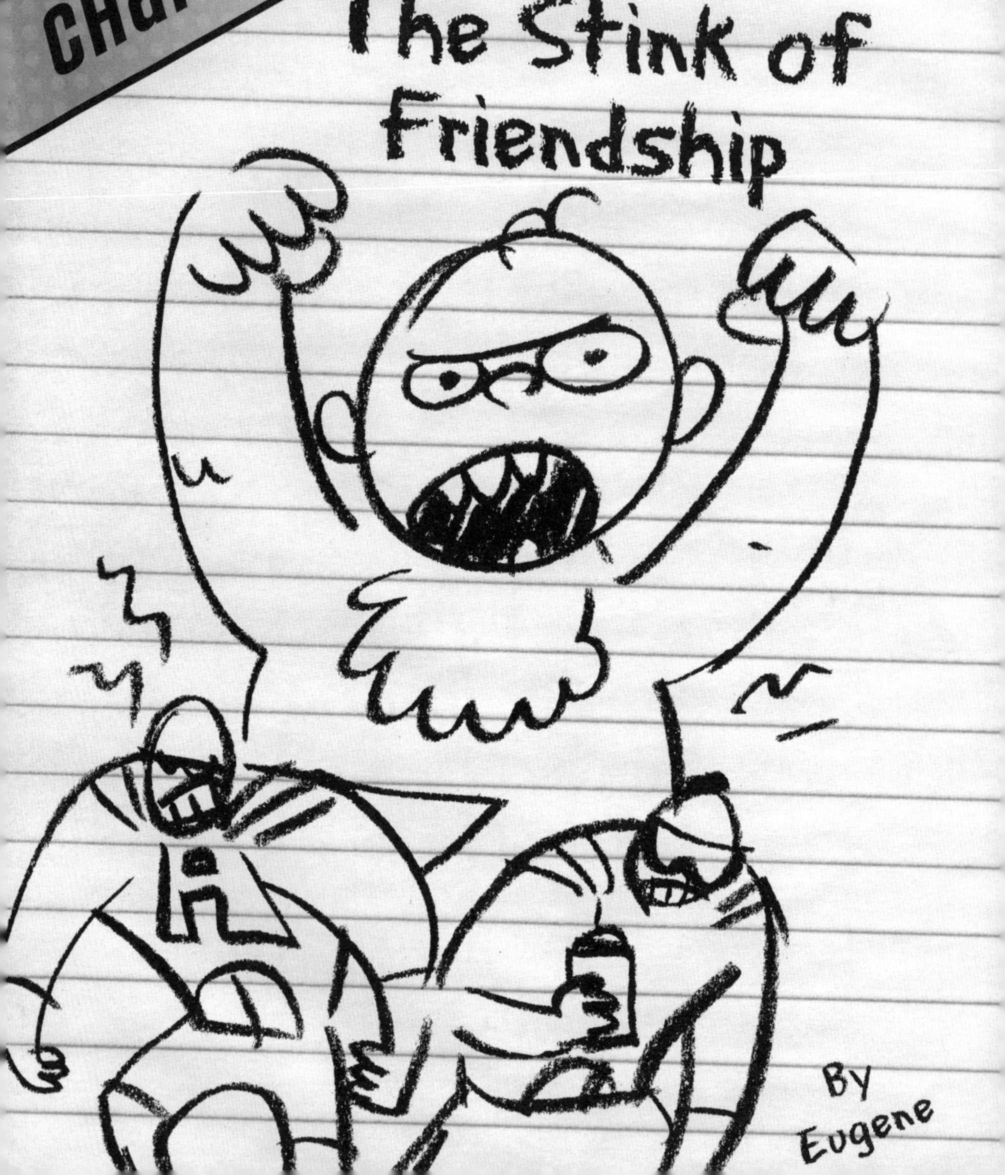

The next morning Eugene and Charlie both woke with a start.

"HOOOOWWWWWWL!"

"Charlie! Mr. Drools is back!" Eugene gasped and quickly reached under his pillow to make sure Super Dude No. 429 was still there.

"I'm all cheesed up and ready to go!" Charlie whipped out two cans of cheese and popped the tops.

ZIP! ZIP!

In a flash the boys pulled out their superhero outfits, and a moment later, Captain Awesome, Nacho Cheese Man, and Turbo—in his plastic hamster ball, the Turbomobile—climbed down the ladder to do battle with the droolicious Mr. Drools!

They jumped off the ladder and onto the surface of the moon, only to be met by the shocking sounds of gibberish!

"Gah-gwarr-goo-gee! *GAAAH!*"

"Oh no!" Nacho Cheese Man cried out, holding his canned cheese even tighter. "It's Queen Stinkypants!"

Eugene was about to unleash some awesome Captain Awesome awesomeness on his archenemy, but then he remembered what his dad had said.

"I . . . I think she just wants to play with us—I mean, fight evil with us," Captain Awesome said, just in time to stop Nacho Cheese

Man from launching his three-cheese attack. "We can always use some extra hero-power to defeat Mr. Drools!"

Queen Stinkypants was going to help them? Nacho Cheese Man was confused for a second. Then he realized Super Dude's famous Rule 42:

Sometimes evil teams up with goodness to fight a bigger evil.

Maybe it was like that with Mr. Drools and Queen Stinkypants. After all, the slobbering menace did gobble up the queen's favorite

Stinkdoll just last week.

Captain Awesome stuck out a hand to Queen Stinkypants and asked, "Do you want to help us?"

"Gwaaa-ha-ha-ha-heee-giggle-giggle!" Queen Stinkypants laughed with joy and she hugged Captain Awesome's leg.

"No hugging." The Captain blushed and quickly unpeeled her.

"HOOOOWWWWWWWL!"

"Come on, heroes! Let's put Mr. Drools back in the doghouse!" Captain Awesome called out and led the charge.

There was a strange smile on Queen Stinkypants's face as the three heroes rushed into battle. There was an even stranger smell coming from her diaper. Captain Awesome knew he might not be able to trust her forever, but at least on this day, they were

three heroes fighting side by side against . . . **THE DREADED MR. DROOLS AND HIS PAWS OF DESTRUCTION—** and Eugene wouldn't have it any other way.

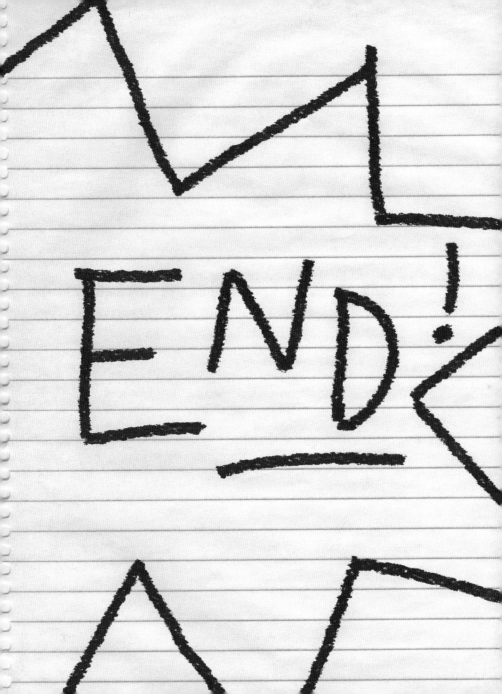

THE END!

CAPTAIN AWESOME

BAM!

COLLECT THEM ALL!

Set of 6 Hardcover Books ISBN: 978-1-5321-4198-0

**Hardcover Book ISBN
978-1-5321-4199-7**

**Hardcover Book ISBN
978-1-5321-4200-0**

**Hardcover Book ISBN
978-1-5321-4201-7**

**Hardcover Book ISBN
978-1-5321-4202-4**

**Hardcover Book ISBN
978-1-5321-4203-1**

**Hardcover Book ISBN
978-1-5321-4204-8**